MONKEY SEE, MONKEY DO

A Folktale Retold by ELLIS CREDLE

THOMAS NELSON & SONS

by ELLIS CREDLE

BIG FRAID, LITTLE FRAID
DOWN, DOWN THE MOUNTAIN
TALL TALES FROM THE HIGH HILLS
MEXICO: Land of Hidden Treasure
A World Neighbor Book

For
Bart & Joyce

1589929

There was once a small cabin made of logs. In front of
it was the ocean. All around the other sides stood
tall pine trees. They were hung with long gray beards
of moss that waggled in the wind.

Inside this small house lived the Cullifers. They were not a very gay family.
Pa Cullifer was glum, Ma was gloomy, big brother Dave was cross, and little brother Chubby was sad. That was because there was no one to talk to, no one to play with. The ocean and the big dark woods were all around and no one lived nearby.

Then, one day something happened to change all this.

Pa and big brother Dave had just pushed off
to go fishing. Little brother Chub was
catching crabs for dinner. He had just caught a
big one when he happened to look out toward
the ocean.

There in the bay a big ship was anchored. A
small boat was coming in from the ship.
A man sat in it, rowing and rowing it nearer
and nearer.

"It's Uncle Bill!" cried little Chub, who was
very fond of his sailor uncle. He always watched
for his ship to pass.

"Ahoy there, little Chub, ahoy!" sang out
Uncle Bill.

"Ahoy, Uncle Bill!" Chub ran to meet him.
Uncle Bill lifted a big basket and stepped ashore.
"Little Chub," he said. "I've brought you a present."
"A present!" exclaimed Chub. "In the basket?"
"Yep, in here. It's a basket full of fun. It's a basket full of laughs."

"What's in it, what's in it?" Chub bounced up and down.

"Truth is," said Uncle Bill as he set the basket down, "everybody on the ship was having so much fun with this present that the Captain got mad. He said the men weren't doing their work. He sent me ashore to— to get rid of—well, I thought of all you Cullifers alone here in the gloomy woods. Just the thing to cheer them up, I said to myself. So here's your present. Open it up!"

Chub opened the basket.

A funny little head popped up.

"It's a monkey!" shouted Chub. "Thank you, Uncle Bill."
The monkey held out his paw. Chub shook it politely.

"His name is Monk. Well, good-by now." Uncle Bill
jumped into his boat and quickly rowed back to the ship.

Just then, along came Dave with a string of fish. When he saw the monkey, how his eyes popped! He was overjoyed with Chub's new pet.

They ran along home, calling to Ma, "Come see, come see what we've got!"

Ma came running. "Oh, my," she frowned. "This means trouble!"

"Trouble?" Chub looked worried.

"Monkeys are such copycats," Ma said. "Whatever they see you do, they try to do the same. Monkey see, monkey do! But they get all mixed up and turn things topsy-turvy." But when Monk put out his paw to shake hands, she took it and smiled.

"Well, at least he's a polite little monkey." Then she went back to the molasses pudding she was beating up for dinner.

When Monk saw her beating and beating the pudding, he got a big spoon and tried to do the same. But his foot slipped. Into the pudding he went head and ears.

What a to-do! He kicked and splashed the pudding all over everything. Ma and the boys had a time fishing him out.

Ma dunked Monk into a tub full of water. She gave him
a bath. Then she hung him on the clothesline to dry.

He sat up in a daze. "What was that?" Pa muttered.
"Did a tree fall down?"

"No, no!" Ma helped him up. "Bill brought Chub a present. It's a—"

"A monkey, a trouble-making monkey!" Pa's eyes lit upon Monk. "Well, we don't want Bill's present." He rubbed his head where a big lump was swelling.

"Now, Pa, don't get riled. We're going to have a nice molasses pudding for dinner," Ma said. "Chubby, you run along now. Bring some wood to make a fire under the pot. We'll have Pa's pudding done in no time."

That made Pa feel better.

Chub went out to the woodpile. He picked up an armful of wood.

When Monk saw what Chub was doing, right away he
wanted to pick up wood too. But instead of carrying it
to the house as Chub did, he ran up a tree and—

threw the wood every which way.

It fell into the chicken yard below. It broke down the fence. It terrified the hens and frightened the roosters.

What a squawking! Through the fence and into the dark woods the silly things flew.

"Quick!" cried Ma. "We must get them or the varmints will catch them and eat them up."

Everybody ran into the woods. When Monk saw them
running to save the chickens, he wanted to go too. He
ran after them. He went peering here and there
among the trees.

Ma and Pa and the boys soon found all the chickens
and got them safely home. Then they looked around for
Monk. Where was he?

"He's lost in the woods!" cried Chub in alarm. "I must find him." He ran this way and that way and saw only big trees. How could he ever find Monk? Then, he spied his pet wandering far ahead.

"Oh, Monk, here, come here!" shouted Chub.

But just then a wolf jumped at Monk from the bushes.

Quickly Monk swung into a tree.

Oh, horrors! A puma was waiting to catch him. Monk jumped from the tree, but down below he met a bear.

Poor Monk, he was too frightened to hear Chub calling. He ran away from the bear as fast as he could go. He jumped on a log floating in the swamp.

The log crawled out of the water. It was a huge old alligator and very hungry. Monk escaped his big jaws just in time. He was terrified.

"Monk! Oh, Monk," called Chub. This time
Monk came running. Chub seized his paw.
"Home," said Chub. "We'll go home."

But which way was home? The tall trees made
dark paths away and away. Monk and Chub
ran along one, then another. Where, oh where
was the little log house?

Then, far and faint they heard, "Chub—ee, Monk—ee, where are you?"

Monk gave a joyful squeak. Chub shouted, "Here, here!"

Then Ma and Pa and Dave were there. How happy they were to find Chub and Monk!

But on the way home Pa said crossly, "A whole day gone and no work done!" He gave Monk a look.

The next day Pa hitched the mule to the sledge and they
all went out to the field where the sweet potatoes grew.
They began to dig the potatoes and throw them onto
the sledge. They dug and dug potatoes until the sledge
was full. Monk wanted to dig potatoes too. But instead of
throwing them onto the sledge, he threw them at the mule.

The mule ran away. What a sight! He kicked
up his heels and the potatoes went flying
every which way.

The Cullifers tried to find the potatoes. They
searched among the bushes. They rooted
among the weeds. But the sun was setting and
they could not see to spy them out.

"Another day wasted!" Pa frowned. "Just
wait until that ship puts in again. We'll see what
happens to this pest of a monkey." He
turned and stared out toward the ocean.

"Aha!" He suddenly pointed. "There she is."

The others looked. There, sailing very close
to shore was Uncle Bill's ship.

Pa cupped his hands, "Ahoy, ship ahoy!" he
bawled.

He grabbed poor Monk and ran down to the shore.

"Wait, wait!" called all the others. "What are you going to do with our Monk?"

Pa paid them no mind. He strode on carrying Monk to the shore and waving to the ship.

Slowly the ship turned about. A small boat was lowered. In it was Uncle Bill. He rowed and rowed for land.

"What's up?" Uncle Bill called.

"Come get your monkey," Pa shouted back. "We've had enough of him!"

Bill beached the boat. He looked glum. "The captain won't like it. He'll put him in irons."

"I don't care." Pa handed Monk aboard.

Uncle Bill rowed slowly out to sea. Monk waved sadly. Ma and Dave and Chub stood crying to see Monk go. Slowly the Cullifers drove the sledge home. The forest seemed bigger and darker. It seemed lonelier than ever.

As the Cullifers sat down to supper, the wind began to whistle around the chimney.

"Just listen. It must be blowing up a storm at sea," Pa said.

The trees began to bend and roar as the wind rushed through them.

"Poor Monk!" said Ma.

"Maybe he'll be shipwrecked," groaned Dave.

"Maybe he'll be lost at sea," moaned Chub.

Nobody felt like eating the good turtle stew that Ma had made. They did not want their corn bread. Pa said the coffee didn't taste good. How sad they felt!

The next morning the wind stopped blowing. The Cullifers set off early to find the potatoes. Dave was cross, Ma was gloomy, Pa looked glum.

Chub sighed, "I wish we had our Monk back." He turned and looked toward the sea. What a surprise!

"Look," he shouted. "Uncle Bill's ship. She's still anchored in the bay!"

Pa stared. "She didn't sail!" he exclaimed. "The wind was blowing too hard."

"Our Monk's still here," said Chub. "Oh, Pa, let's get him back."

"Oh, Pa, let's get Monk back," said Ma.

"Please, please," begged Chub and Dave.

Pa looked bothered. "It's too late," he said. "Just look, the ship is hoisting her sails. She's going."

They all ran down to the shore. Ma took off her shawl.
She flung it up and down. Pa waved his red handkerchief.
Dave waved his hat. Chub waved his arms.

No one on the ship saw the Cullifers waving and screaming. The sails slowly filled with wind and the ship headed out to sea.

"Quick, let's row after her," said Chub.

They all jumped into the rowboat. Each one, even Pa, grabbed an oar. Oh, how they rowed! They reached the ship just as she was picking up speed.

"Ahoy, ahoy there, Bill," yelled Pa.

Bill came to the rail. So did the Captain and all the sailors.

"We want our Monk," called the Cullifers. "We want our Monk again."

"With the greatest of pleasure," the Captain called down.

Quickly a rope ladder was thrown over the side. Down came Monk. The big ship went up and down, up and down with the waves.

What fun! Monk went swinging and swinging on the ladder. Then he gave a leap toward the Cullifers' boat. Just then the big ship went up. This made Monk fly clean over the little boat.

Splash! He fell into the sea.

The Cullifers fished him out. Pa dried him with his handkerchief. Ma wrapped him in her shawl. They rowed him ashore.

Quickly they put him to bed. Ma put a mustard plaster on his chest. Pa brought a bowl of hot soup. Chub made him a cup of sassafras tea. Dave brought another quilt.

The next morning Monk was fine. The Cullifers were happy to have him back home again. They never felt lonely any more for Monk kept them busy laughing all the time. He did so many tricks that people are still telling tales about him.

About the Author

ELLIS CREDLE grew up in the lowlands of North Carolina, the locale of many of her books. After her graduation from Louisburg College, she taught school in the Blue Ridge Mountains. Out of that experience came her first published story, *Down, Down the Mountain*, now a classic among books for children.

In 1925, Ellis Credle went to New York to study art in preparation for a career in interior decorating. Commissioned to paint the murals for the Children's Museum in Brooklyn, she became interested in juvenile literature and has since written many books for children of all ages.

On a voyage to South America, Miss Credle met Charles Townsend, a well-known photographer, who later became her husband and worked with her on several books—illustrating them with his camera.

For the past twenty years, Ellis Credle and her husband have made Guadalajara their home. The World Neighbor book *Mexico: Land of Hidden Treasure* is a warm interpretation of her adopted country, an attempt to prepare the way for an understanding of this enlightened, exotically romantic neighbor to the south.

At present, one of Ellis Credle's main interests is the collecting and adapting of old folktunes, which she sings, accompanying herself on a guitar.